A Shadow of Affection

Arigato Sensei

BLUEROSE PUBLISHERS
India | U.K.

Copyright © Arigato Sensei 2025

All rights reserved by author. No part of this publication may be reproduced, stored in a retrieval system or transmitted in any form or by any means, electronic, mechanical, photocopying, recording or otherwise, without the prior permission of the author. Although every precaution has been taken to verify the accuracy of the information contained herein, the publisher assumes no responsibility for any errors or omissions. No liability is assumed for damages that may result from the use of information contained within.

BlueRose Publishers takes no responsibility for any damages, losses, or liabilities that may arise from the use or misuse of the information, products, or services provided in this publication.

For permissions requests or inquiries regarding this publication, please contact:

BLUEROSE PUBLISHERS
www.BlueRoseONE.com
info@bluerosepublishers.com
+91 8882 898 898
+4407342408967

ISBN: 978-93-6452-671-5

First Edition: June 2025

llo name is Yug
a normal
overt guy in
overt family

who used to always get scold on me for my shyness and less talking with everyone and I don't like to talk with people I like watching anime and reading manga at home alone

I don't like social life or people very much and I am a th student of class 11 with pcm streams yaa I like maths it's not usual that people like maths but that's tha way just I am

In the enchanting realm of Nara City, where cherry blossoms dance on the breeze, a young introvert named Yug led a solitary life. His heart, inseparable from the pages of manga and the captivating world of anime, yearned to experience the magic beyond the confines of his bedroom walls

g possessed a unique gift, ert one that troubled him atly. He suffered from a mplex condition known as ltiple personality disorder, using fragments of his own ntity to splinter and intertwine. wever, his warm and gentle ure remained dominant, spite the fragmented abyss hin.

starting chapter 1 pg1

yug has some animal

dog name Band

they have a big aquarium. In aquarium they have turtle and some fish

chapter 1 pg5

Yug sits in his seat.

Blushing! he hides and looks at the arrow

Yug finds out while studying himself and he realises that he is trying to become better as if he is not good yet

there are two reasons for this

The first reason is that Yug has made a promise to his mom

The second reason is that I want to get tension from my crush and I want to impress her by getting a little more marks than her.

he decreased the time he spent on anime manga and smart phone

chapter 1 pg11

to be continue with chapter 2

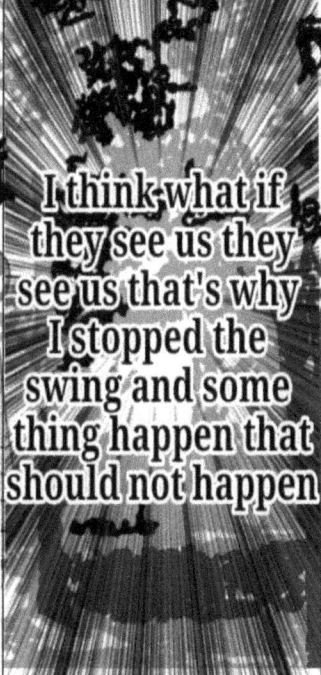

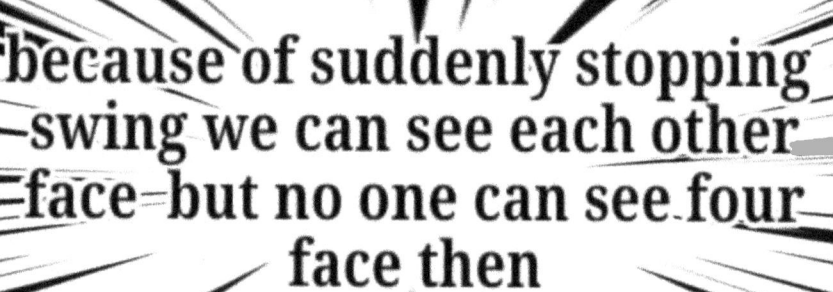

chapter 2 pg7

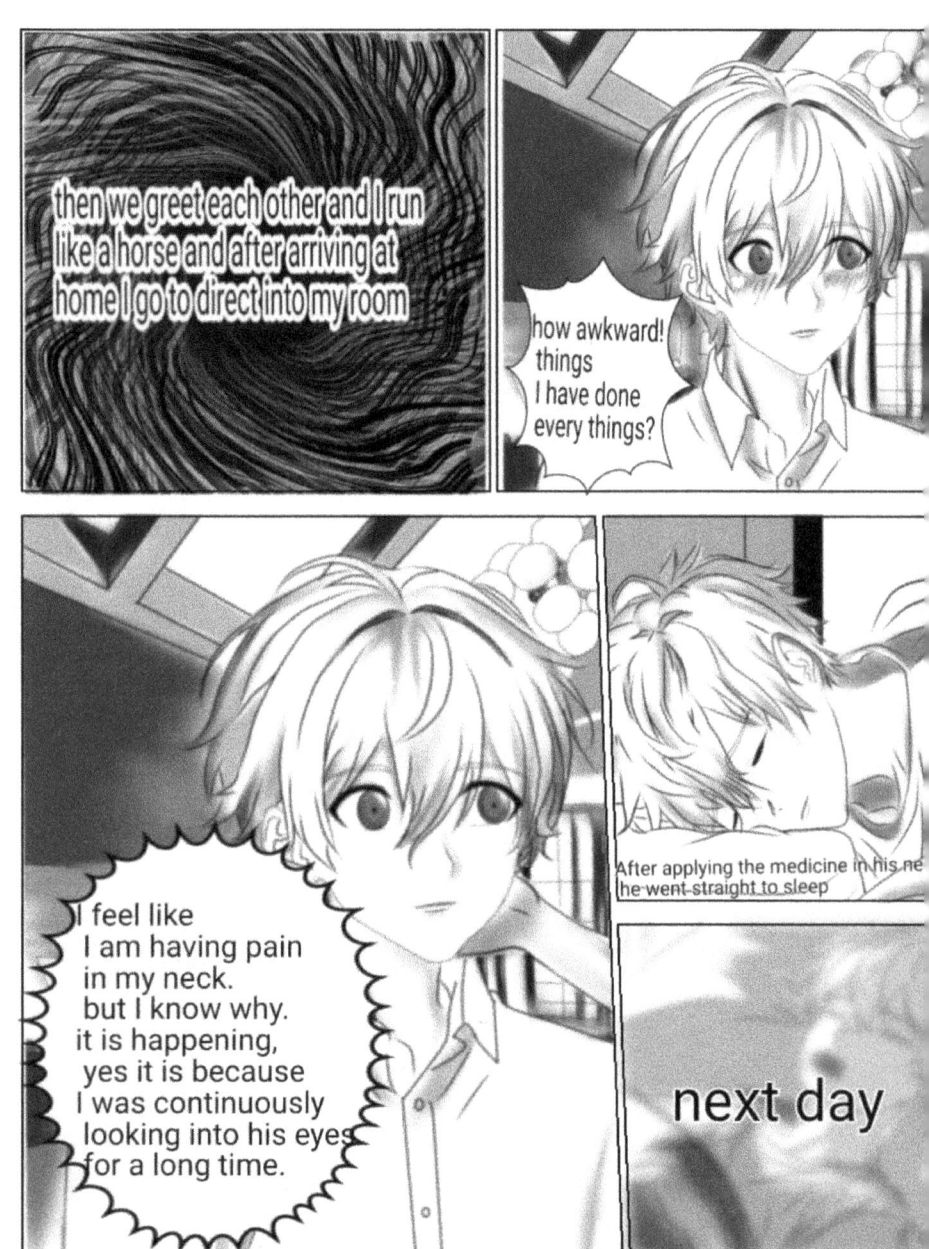

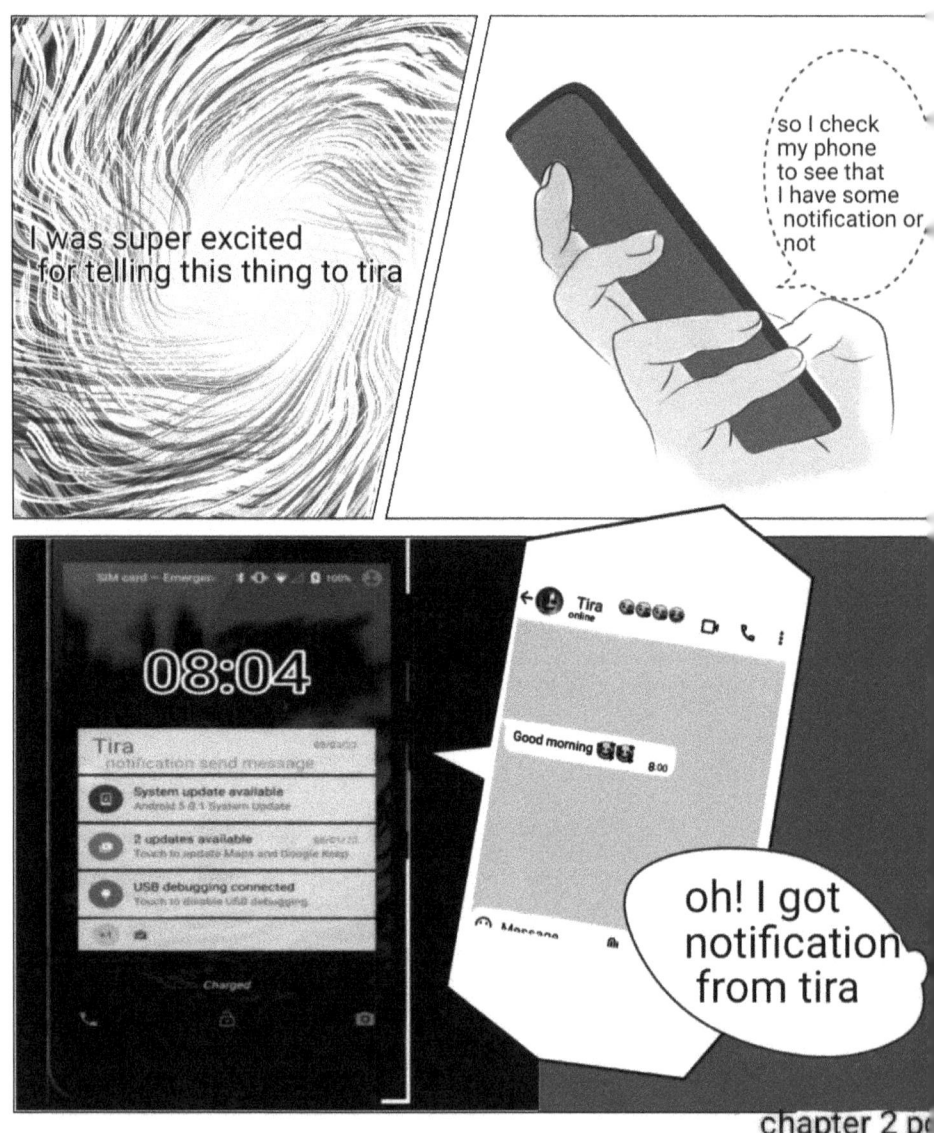

my family members noticed that I have doing more study then deform

Although I used to read manga often

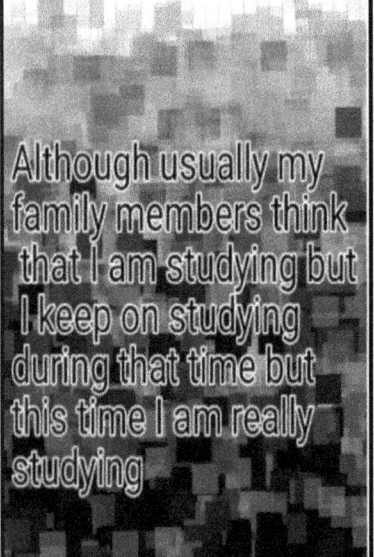

Although usually my family members think that I am studying but I keep on studying during that time but this time I am really studying

good luck ⊂(•‿•)⊃

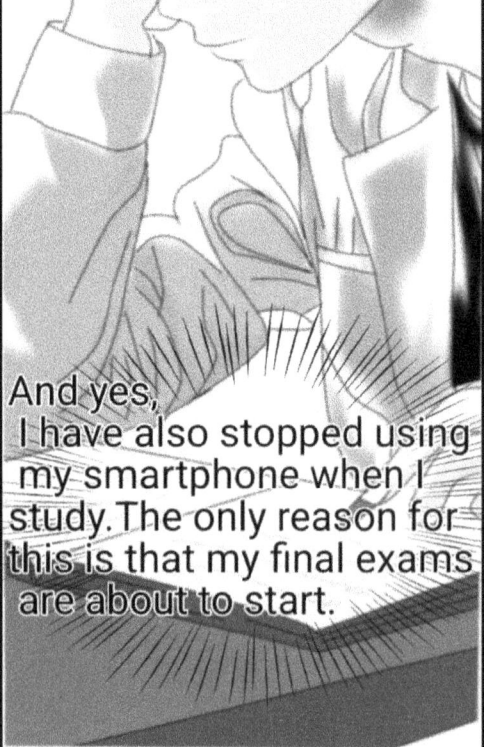

And yes, I have also stopped using my smartphone when I study. The only reason for this is that my final exams are about to start.

chapter 2 pg15

to be continue
 with
chapter 3

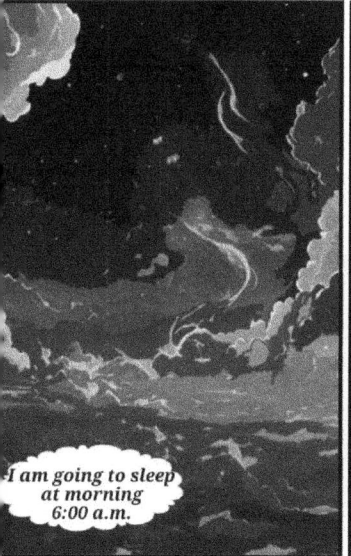

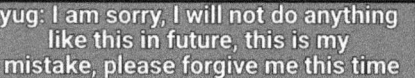

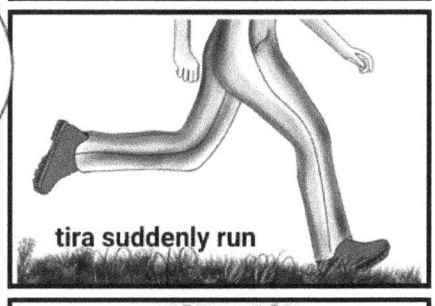

chapter 3 page 11

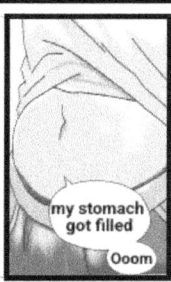

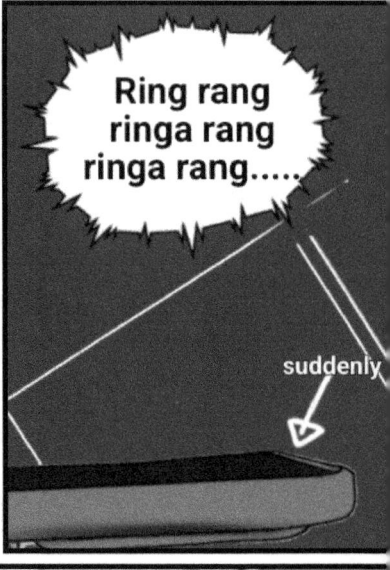

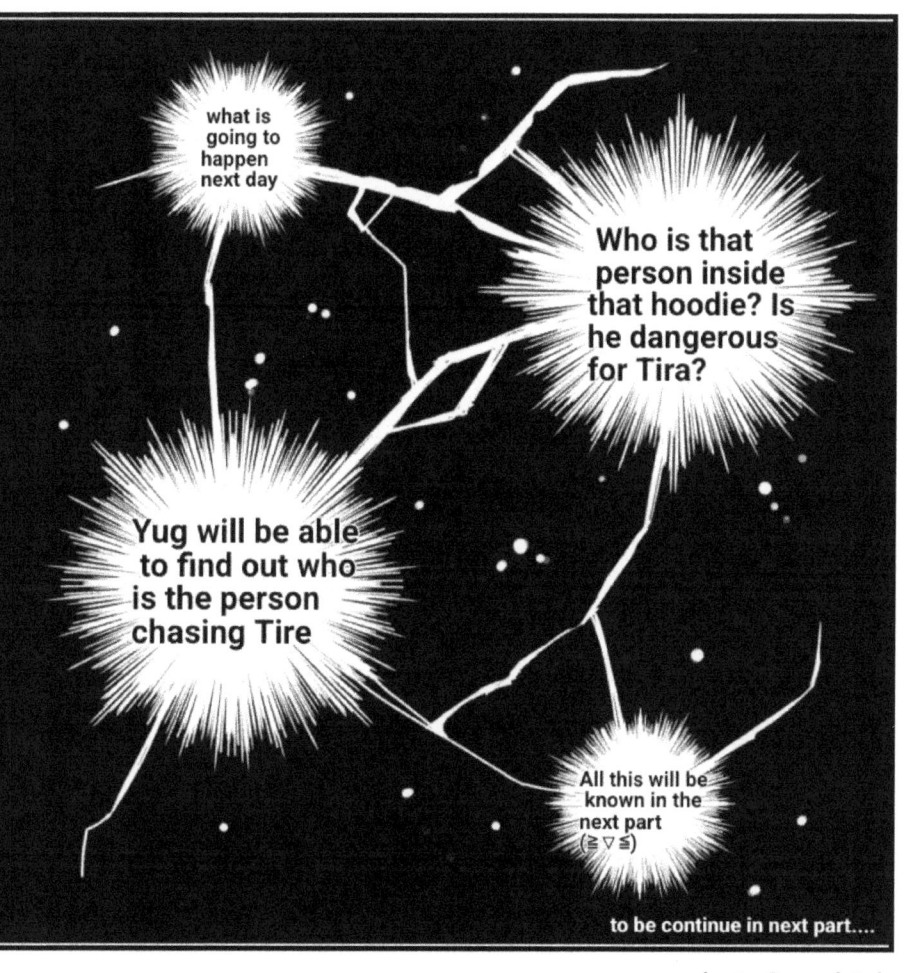

www.ingramcontent.com/pod-product-compliance
Lightning Source LLC
LaVergne TN
LVHW061622070526
838199LV00078B/7388